Animal Masquerade

Marianne Dubuc

Kids Can Press

Come one, come all
to the animal masquerade.

Disguises are a must!

The lion didn't know how he should disguise himself ...

As a cat?
As a chicken?
As a toad?
As ...

An elephant!

The elephant went disguised as ...

A parrot.

The parrot went disguised as ...

A turtle.

The turtle went disguised as ...

Little Red Riding Hood.

Little Red Riding Hood went disguised as ...

A chocolate cake.

Uh-oh!
The bear has quite
a sweet tooth.

Be careful,
Little Red Riding Hood!

But the bear was
much
too
s l o w .

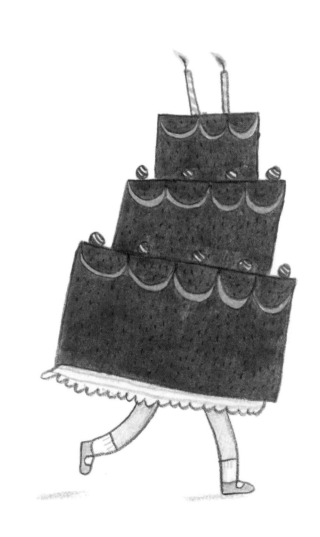

He was a real slowpoke.

So the bear went disguised as ...

A snail.

The snail went disguised as ...

A tiger.

The tiger went disguised as ...

A soft white sheep.

The soft white sheep went disguised as ...

I'm prickly!

A porcupine.

The porcupine went disguised as ...

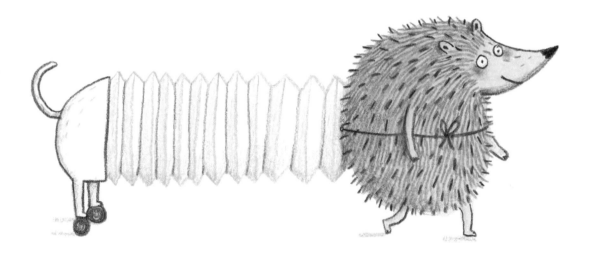

A wiener dog.

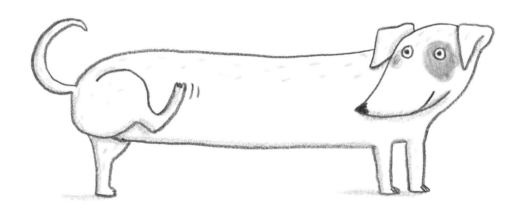

The wiener dog went disguised as ...

A **zebra**.

The zebra went disguised as ...

A mouse.

The mouse went disguised as ...

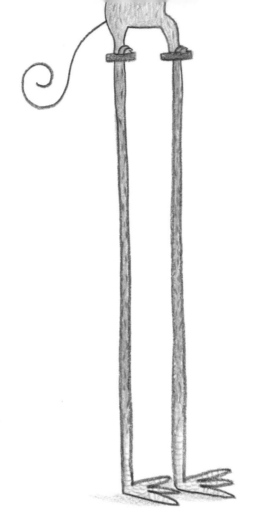

A pink flamingo.

The pink flamingo went disguised as …

A giraffe.

The giraffe went disguised as ...

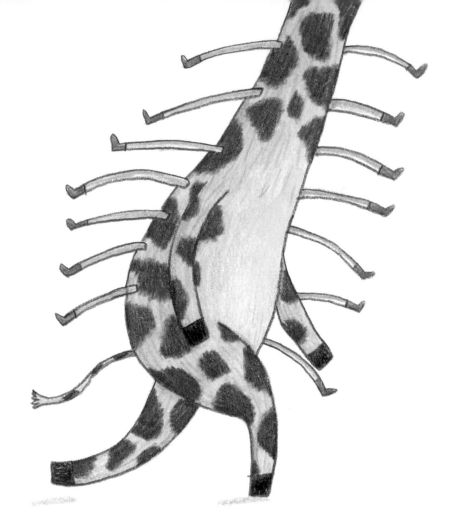

A millipede.

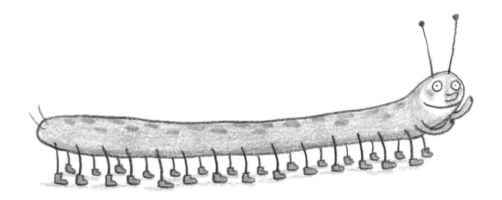

The millipede went disguised as ...

A teeny-tiny fish.

The teeny-tiny fish went disguised as ...

That

makes

A cat.

catfish!

a

him

The cat went disguised as ...

A crocodile.

The crocodile went disguised as ...

A dromedary.

The dromedary went disguised as ...

A ca**m**el.

That's too easy!

The camel went disguised as ...

A polar bear.

The polar bear went disguised as ...

A swan.

The swan and her two cygnets went disguised as ...

The Three Little Pigs.

The Three Little Pigs went disguised as ...

A **grumbly** rhinoceros.

The grumbly rhinoceros, who is actually very nice, went disguised as ...

A sweet yellow chick.

The sweet yellow chick went disguised as ...

A hairy-legged spider.

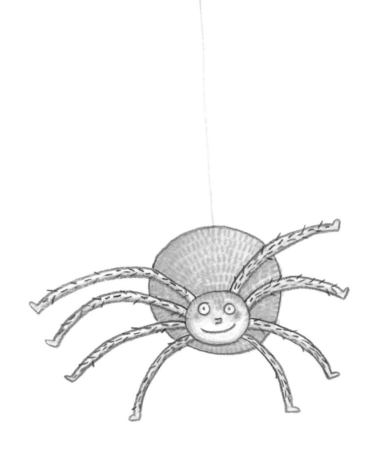

The hairy-legged spider went disguised as ...

A skunk.

The skunk, who is a bit stinky,
went disguised as ...

A *pretty* poppy.

The pretty poppy went disguised as ...

Flowers don't wear disguises, but they smell **very** good.

So it was the ladybug that went disguised as ...

A hippopotamus.

The hippopotamus went disguised as ...

An armadillo.

The armadillo went disguised as ...

A lobster.

The lobster went disguised as ...

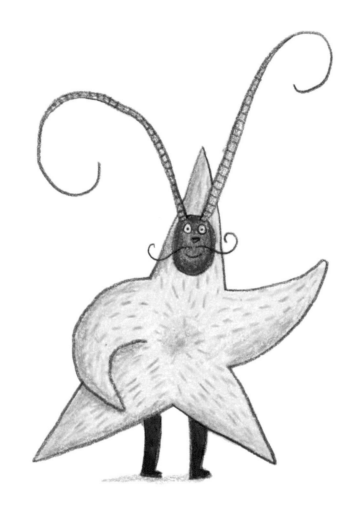

A starfish.

The starfish went disguised as ...

A sleek **black** panther.

The sleek black panther went disguised as ...

A racc●●n.

The raccoon went disguised as ...

A fox.

The fox went disguised as ...

A hen.

The hen went disguised as ...

The hen
didn't dress up.

She didn't understand a thing.
(She isn't very smart.)

The cow, the hare and the chipmunk
went disguised as ...

A **scary** three-headed monster.

The scary three-headed monster
went disguised as ...

A tiny **marmoset.**

The tiny marmoset went disguised as ...

Hop!

A frog.

The frog went disguised as ...

A bull.

That makes him
a bullfrog!

The bull went disguised as ...

A rattlesnake.

The rattlesnake went disguised as ...

A unicorn.

The unicorn went disguised as ...

A hummingbird.

The hummingbird went disguised as ...

An ostrich

The ostrich went disguised as ...

A butterfly.

The butterfly went disguised as ...

A bat.

The bat went disguised as ...

A **big** gorilla.

The big gorilla went disguised as ...

A mama kangaroo.

The mama kangaroo went disguised as ...

A **pudgy** panda.

The pudgy panda went disguised as ...

A platypus.

The platypus went disguised as ...

The platypus
didn't dress up.

He looks like he's already
in disguise.

Welcome to the masquerade!

To you, to whom I owe everything — M.D.

Originally published under the title *Au carnaval des animaux* by Les éditions de la courte échelle inc.

Text and illustrations © 2011 Les éditions de la courte échelle inc.
English translation © 2012 Kids Can Press
English translation by Yvette Ghione

Kids Can Press acknowledges the financial support of the Government of Ontario, through the Ontario Media Development Corporation's Ontario Book Initiative; the Ontario Arts Council; the Canada Council for the Arts; and the Government of Canada, through the BPIDP, for our publishing activity.

Published in Canada by	Published in the U.S. by
Kids Can Press Ltd.	Kids Can Press Ltd.
25 Dockside Drive	2250 Military Road
Toronto, ON M5A 0B5	Tonawanda, NY 14150

www.kidscanpress.com

The artwork in this book was rendered in pencil crayon.
The text is set in Absent Grotesque.

Original edition edited by Anne-Sophie Tilly and Lise Duquette
English edition edited by Yvette Ghione
Designed by Mathieu Lavoie

This book is smyth sewn casebound.
Manufactured in Singapore, in 10/2011 by Tien Wah Press (Pte) Ltd.

CM 12 0 9 8 7 6 5 4 3 2 1

Library and Archives Canada Cataloguing in Publication

Dubuc, Marianne, 1980-
Animal masquerade / Marianne Dubuc.

Translation of: Au carnaval des animaux.
ISBN 978-1-55453-782-2

1. Animals–Pictorial works–Juvenile literature. I. Title.

QL49.D8213 2012   j590.22'2   C2011-904723-3

Kids Can Press is a /orus™ Entertainment company